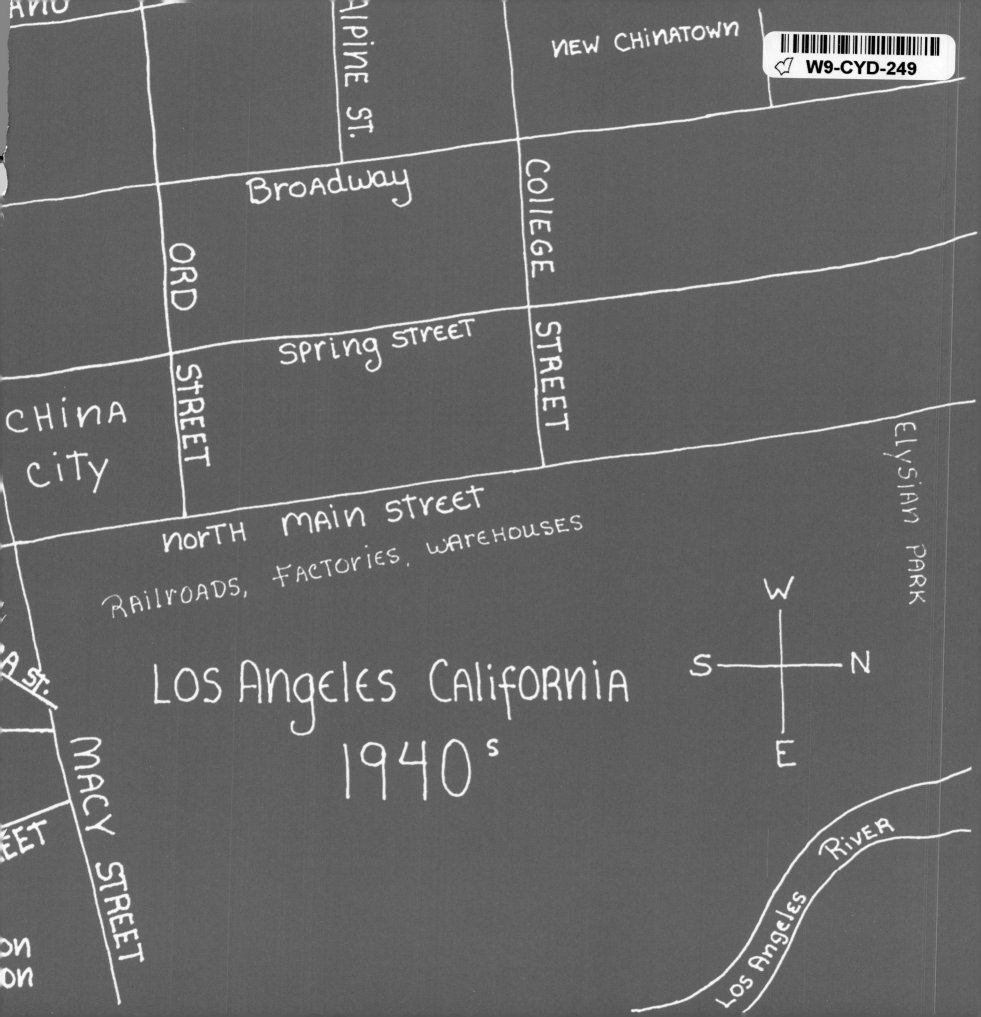

Enjoy this fascinating history!

[signature]

June 25, 2012

$1.50

MEI LING IN CHINA CITY

チャイナ・シティのメイリンちゃん

WRITTEN BY ICY SMITH

ILLUSTRATED BY GAYLE GARNER ROSKI

アイシー・スミス作　ゲイル・ガーナー・ロスキ画

Japanese translation by Sunny Seki　サニー関訳 (せきやく)

East West Discovery Press
Manhattan Beach, California

It has been three years since we moved to Los Angeles Chinatown from Oregon. Now we live in a small house on Alpine Street. My parents told me that the original Los Angeles Chinatown, called Old Chinatown, was demolished not long ago to build Union Station, the main train station in Los Angeles. In 1938, thousands of Chinese Americans were forced to relocate to other Chinese communities, and they were not treated very respectfully. Some moved to the area around City Market on 9th and San Pedro Streets, and some moved to the newly built China City and New Chinatown where we live. My family owns and runs a Chinese restaurant called Chung Dat Loo in China City where I waitress after school almost every day.

私 がオレゴンからロサンジェルスのチャイナタウンに引っ越してきて、三年がたちました。今、私 の家族はアルパイン通りの小さな家に住んでいます。両親 の話 では、旧 チャイナタウンは、少し前にロサンジェルスの主要駅、ユニオン・ステーションを建てるために取りこわされたそうです。１９３８年のその時には、何千人もの中国 系アメリカ人が強制的 にほかの中国人 の住む地域へと移されました。追い出された人たちは, サンペドロ通りと九番街 、市営マーケットのあるあたりや、今、私 たちが住んでいる、新 しいチャイナ・シティへと分散したのです。私 の家族はそこで、「チャング・ダット・ルー」という名の中華レストランを開いているので、私 は学校から帰ると、毎日のようにウエイトレスをします。

MAIN STREET

MACY STREET

SPRING STREET

CHINA CITY

ORD STREET

This year, I am sad in school. I lost my best friend Yayeko Akiyama, who was sent to the Manzanar internment camp with her family. Last December 1941, after Pearl Harbor was attacked by Japan, the U.S. government forced thousands of Japanese Americans out of their homes and sent them to ten different War Relocation Centers across the country. Rumors say that the U.S. government might use them as hostages against the Japanese invasion. I don't understand why the government is treating the Japanese Americans differently. Yayeko is American like me. It is just because her ancestors were born in Japan. Most of the Japanese internees are U.S. citizens, and didn't commit any crime against the country. Since she went away, we write letters to each other, but I wish I could see her in person.

今年は、学校で悲しい出来事がありました。親友だったアキヤマ・ヤエコちゃんが家族と共に、マンザナーの日系人戦時収容所へ送られ、もう会えなくなってしまったのです。去年、１９４１年の１２月、日本が真珠湾を攻撃すると、アメリカ政府は多くの日系人を強制的に立ち退かせ、国内に十ヶ所あった収容所に入れたのです。もし日本軍が上陸したら、アメリカ政府は彼らを人質として対抗するという噂です。私には政府が日系人になぜ、そんなひどい扱いをするのかわかりません。ヤエコちゃんは私と同じアメリカ人だというのに。ただ先祖が日本人というだけの理由です。多くの日系収容者はアメリカ市民で、国に対して何の罪も犯していないのです。収容されてしまった彼女と文通するようになりましたが、直接会えたら、どんなにかうれしいでしょう。

July 15, 1942

Dear Mei Ling,

Life is very difficult in this camp. I'm so bored. Manzanar is in a dry, windy desert with dust and sand everywhere. I wake up every morning with dust on my face. The Sierra Nevada Mountains create a high wall behind our camp, and I can see snow up there. The camp has a four-mile barbed wire fence around it with armed guards. There are guards in eight high watchtowers with their guns pointing inward toward us. We live in a crowded military-style barrack, eat in noisy mess hall with everyone else, and share the latrine and shower rooms. There is no privacy at all. I heard a few schools will be opened up here soon, but none have opened yet. I hope I don't get too far behind. But school will not be fun without you. I miss you and the good times we had. Did you make any new friends? Write to me soon.

Love,

Yayeko Akiyama

Manzanar, California

１９４２年７月１５日

親愛なるメイリンちゃんへ

収容所の生活には全く気落ちしてしまいます。本当にうんざり。収容所の背後には、シェラ・ネバダ山脈が高い壁のようにそびえて、上の方に雪が見えます。四マイルの長い鉄条網が収容所をぐるりと囲み、武装した守衛がいます。銃を私たちに向けた高い監視塔が八つあって、看守が見張っているのです。私たちは兵舎のような小屋に詰め込まれて住み、騒がしい食堂でほかの人と一緒に食べ、土を掘ったトイレと浴場は共同で使います。プライバシーは全くありません。いくつか学校が開設される予定ですが、まだ何の連絡もありません。はやく学校の授業に追いつきたいと願っています。だけど、メイリンちゃんと一緒でない中学校じゃあつまらない。ふたりで過ごした思い出がなつかしいです。新しい友達はできましたか？　すぐ返事を下さいね。

愛をこめて

ヤエコ

マンザナー、カリフォルニア州

Mom says, "The Moon Festival celebration is tomorrow and I want you to wear your silk dress. Only traditional Chinese clothes tomorrow, dear."

I go to my closet and pull out my long, red silk dress with yellow flowers hand embroidered on it. The last time I wore this was with Yayeko during the Chinese New Year festival last year. I try it on and it still fits me perfectly, but I am growing and this is likely the last time I will wear it. I remember last year walking down the street with my grandmother, who has bound feet, holding on to my arm. I am so happy that I was not born in China, where many girls' and women's feet were forced to fit into shoes about three inches long called lotus shoes. My grandmother told me that in the upper classes in China, foot binding usually began when a girl was three years old. A good marriage would be impossible to arrange if the girl had big ugly feet.

ママの声がします。「メイリン、あしたはムーン・フェスティバルよ。絹のドレスに着替えなさい。中国の昔からの習慣だからね」
　　わたしはタンスから絹の長くて赤い、黄色の花模様が刺繍してあるドレスを取り出します。前にこの服を着たのは、去年の中国の新年祝賀祭のときで、ヤエコちゃんも一緒でした。着てみるとぴったりでしたが、私も大きくなってきたので、この服を着られるのも、今年が最後でしょう。去年、それを着た時に、足を纏足にしている私のおばあちゃんが、私の手につかまりながら道を歩いたのを思い出しました。私は中国に生まれなくて良かったと思います。だって、多くの少女や女の人たちは、強制的に長さ三インチ位のロータス・シューズと呼ばれる靴をはかされてしまうからです。おばあちゃんの話だと、中国の上流社会で「足かせ」をはめるのは女の子が三歳になるころからで、良い結婚を望んでも、足が大きくては、ぶざまで見込みがないからだそうです。

Lotus Shoes
ロータス・シューズ

Today, we go to the restaurant early in preparation for the big crowd coming to China City. My dad is the main chef of our restaurant and is preparing the many ingredients for our most popular dishes such as Egg Foo Young, Cashew Nut Chicken, Chop Suey, and Fried Rice. They are Chinese American dishes, not really Chinese food, but it still tastes good to me.

"Mei Ling, go to Mr. Ling's gift shop to buy more lanterns. We need to get this place decorated properly," Pa yells to me, "and get a dozen more moon cakes, too."

きょうはチャイナ・シティに大勢の人がくり出して来るので、私の家族は早めに出かけて準備をします。パパはレストランのコック長ですから、お店で人気のエッグフーヤング、鶏肉とカシューナッツ炒め、肉入り野菜炒めや、チャーハンなどの下ごしらえに余念がありません。これらはアメリカ風の中華料理で、純粋の中華料理ではないのですが私も大好きです。

「おーい、メイリン。リングさんのギフトショップへ行って、提灯を少し買ってきておくれ。それらしい飾りつけをしなくちゃ。それと月餅を、もう一ダースほど欲しいな」パパの大きな声が聞こえます。

I walk up the staircase to Lotus Pool Road, passing the Golden Phoenix Restaurant, and stop by the Kuan Yin Temple to visit Johnny Yee. He is a good friend of mine and always has something entertaining to say. As I enter the temple, I immediately smell the fragrant incense and hear the soft chanting made by the Buddhists praying there. Johnny, who is seventeen, five years older than me, is wearing his long, black Chinese robe. This is not his normal outfit, but he says that's what the tourists like to see. He is selling a fortune-telling stick and incense to a passerby. "That'll be seven cents, please." The altar table is decorated with fruits, flowers, roast pig, moon cake, and tea.

蓮池通りへの階段を上り、「ゴールデン・フェニックス」レストランを過ぎて、クワン・イン寺院にジョニー・イーさんがいるかどうか、のぞいてみました。彼はいつも、おもしろいことを言って、楽しませてくれる友達なのです。お寺に入ったとたん、お線香の匂いとお坊さんたちの低い読経の声が聞こえます。ジョニーさんは私より五歳年上で十七歳、長くて黒い中国式礼服を着ています。いつもと違う身なりなのは、彼によると観光客を喜ばすためなんですって。彼は「七セントですよー」と行き交う人に声をかけ、おみくじの棒とお線香を売っています。聖壇にはくだもの、花、焼き豚、月餅そしてお茶が供えられ、美しく飾られています。

"Good morning, Johnny. Are you going to perform the lion dance in the parade today?" I ask.

"Yep, of course. Our troupe can't perform without me," Johnny smiles.

"How about you? You look nice today in your silk dress. Are you working for Mr. Gubbins today?"

Mr. Gubbins is an actors' agent for Asian American talent and has an office and film studio in China City. He specializes in hiring Chinese actors and extras for Hollywood movies. Many people from the neighborhood are recruited to act in movie productions. That is why China City is nicknamed the Chinese Movie Land.

"Not today. I am busy helping out at the restaurant, and in fact I have to get some lanterns right away. I'll see you later today in the parade," I reply.

おはよう、ジョニーさん。きょうのパレードではライオンダンスを踊るの？」 私 が聞きます。

「ああ、もちろんさ。ぼくが出なくちゃダンスの連中 は困まっちゃうからね」 ジョニーさんはにっこりして答えると、こんどは私 に聞き返します。

「それで、メイリンちゃんは何をするの？　きょうは絹のドレスでおめかししているところをみると、ははあガビンスおじさんの仕事をするのかな？」

ガビンスおじさんは、アジア系アメリカ人の俳優の営業 代理人で、チャイナ・シティの中にスタジオを兼ねた事務所をもっています。ハリウッドの映画に出る中国 系の俳優や脇役をやとうのが、おじさんの専門です。となり近所でたくさんの人が映画に出演 するので、チャイナ・シティはチャイニーズ・ムービーランドのニックネームがつきました。

「きょうは違うの。私 はレストランの手伝いで忙 しいし、これから提 灯 を買いに行くの。じゃあ、きょうのパレードの時にまたね」 と答えて別れます。

I run into the Golden Lantern Gift Shop and buy dozens of paper lanterns, then to the Che Kiang Importers for moon cakes. On my way back, I pass through the Court of Lotus Pools and see my friends Ruby, Frances, and Doris. They are holding American flags and have a tin box with the words United China Relief Fundraiser on it. They are collecting money for the people in China suffering because of the war.

"Hi, Mei Ling. Would you like to join us in our fundraising drive today? We're selling Chinese opera tickets and American flags. The top seller will win a $100 Chinese banquet gift certificate and a Chinese silk jacket," Ruby tells me. "We are selling the opera tickets and flags for $1 each. The money raised will help the women and children refugees in China."

"Oh. If you like, I can try to sell the tickets and flags at my parents' restaurant today," I reply.

"Great," says Ruby, as she hands over the flags and another tin box.

In my mind, I hope that the war will end soon so we can reconnect with our family in China, and our Japanese American friends here in the U.S. I hope the sick and displaced Chinese families in China will not suffer any more. I also want to see Yayeko and others come home.

ゴールデン・ランタン・ギフトショップで一ダースの紙提灯と、チェ・キャング輸入店で月餅を買います。帰り道、蓮池のある中庭を通りかかると友達のルビー、フランシスそしてドリスと会いました。アメリカの国旗と総合中国救済募金と書かれたブリキの箱を持っています。彼女たちは戦争で苦しんでいる中国の人々に送るお金を集めているのです。

「ねえ、メイリン。私たちの募金運動を手伝ってくれない？ 中国歌劇の切符とアメリカの国旗を売っているの。一番売り上げた人は、中華料理店のディナー招待券百ドル分と中国製の絹のジャケットがもらえるのよ」ルビーが誘います。「切符と国旗はそれぞれ一ドル、このお金は戦争で傷ついた中国の人々にとって大助かりだと思うわ」

私はそれを聞いて「もし良かったら、きょうその切符と国旗をうちのレストランで売ってみようかしら」と答えました。

「そう来なくっちゃ」と言って、ルビーは国旗の束とブリキの箱を私に手渡します。

私は心の中で、早く戦争が終わって、私たちも中国にいる家族とふたたび行き来できるよう、またアメリカに住む日系人の友達と再会できるよう祈らずにはいられません。どうか中国の病気の人たち、住むところを失った人たちが、これ以上苦しむことがありませんように。ヤエコちゃんや、みんなが一日も早く帰ってきますように。

Back in my restaurant, I help Papa and Mom decorate the lanterns. Very soon, thousands of Southern Californians arrive in China City and gather at the Court of Four Seasons. The lion dance parade and firecrackers kick off the Moon Festival celebration. Some ride the traditional rickshaw for 25 cents. Others browse through the mysterious Chinese village with quaint bazaars, knick-knack stores, lotus pools, temples, and movie sets. Many support the war relief effort by buying American flags and tickets to see "Mulan" and "The Chinese Princess" operas. In China City, it is interesting to see the traditional Chinese operas performed in English only, because most of the audience do not speak Chinese.

Our restaurant is overflowing with customers coming from all over town. I take advantage of the opportunity to sell the tickets and flags to our customers. After the busy lunch time, Ruby comes in to my restaurant with a frown on her face.

レストランにもどると、私 はパパとママを手伝って、提灯 を飾りつけます。しばらくすると、南 カリフォルニア中 からたくさんの人がチャイナ・シティにやって来て、フォーシーズンズの中庭に集合 します。ムーン・フェスティバルは、獅子舞いのパレードと爆竹で幕を開けるのです。二十五セントを払い、昔 ながらの人力車に乗る人もいれば、風変わりな雑貨店、おみやげ屋、蓮の池、お寺、それに映画用のセットなどが並ぶミステリアスな中華街をぶらつく人もいます。かなり多くの人がアメリカ国旗を買い、またチャイナ・シティで催 されている歌劇「ムーラン」や「中国 のプリンセス」の切符を買って、戦争被災者の救済 に協力的 です。おもしろいことに、伝統的な中国 歌劇がここでは英語だけで演じられています。というのは、観客 のほとんどが中国語を話さないからです。

うちのレストランはあちこちから来たお客 さんで混んできました。これは良いチャンス、と切符や旗を売り込みます。忙 しいお昼時を過ぎたところで、ルビーが不満顔でレストランにやってきました。

"How much did you raise so far?" Ruby asks. "Richard, who works at China Burger restaurant, seems to be winning the race. He has raised more than $70. I heard he offers the donors a free cup of coffee with each ticket or flag sold."

"Well, I've sold about $55. I'll think about some ways to sell more," I say. I think to myself, winning the fundraising drive is important to me. Besides helping the war victims, I want to save my prize for Yayeko when she returns home.

The weather is pretty hot today and that gives me an idea. "Hey, Ruby. I usually sell fresh-squeezed orange juice for 10 cents on the weekends. How about I give a free orange juice with each ticket or flag sold?"

"Great, that idea is perfect. I will help you squeeze the oranges," Ruby says with excitement.

Since the busy lunch time has passed, I have Mom's permission to make a fundraising booth just outside the restaurant, offering free cold orange juice.

「どのくらい売れた？」ルビーが聞きます。「チャイナ・バーガーで働いているリチャードが今のところトップの売れ行きだそうよ。もう七十ドルも集めたんだって。彼は切符か旗を買うと、ただでコーヒー一杯をサービスするらしいわ」

私は「えーと、五十五ドルくらい売れたと思うけど。もっと売れる方法がないかしら」と答えながら、この募金コンテストにぜひ勝たなくっちゃ、と思いました。戦争の被害者を救うだけでなく、獲得した賞品をヤエコちゃんがもどってきたら、プレゼントしようと決めたのです。

きょうは暑いなぁと思ったとたん、あるアイデアがひらめきました。「ルビー、あのね、私は週末にフレッシュな絞りたてのオレンジ・ジュースを十セントで売ることがあるの。もし切符か旗を買ってくれれば、ただでオレンジ・ジュースを差し上げます、と言ったらどうなると思う？」

ルビーは大喜びです。「すごい、それは名案よ。私はオレンジを絞るのを手伝うわ」

忙しいお昼の時間が終わっていたので、私はママからレストランの前に、冷たいオレンジ・ジュースを提供する募金用テーブルを出す許可をもらうことができました。

The colorful Moon Festival activities draw thousands of people. In no time, our orange juice stand attracts a long line of thirsty visitors. One familiar face comes to our stand. Ruby and I stare at her for a moment, realizing… it's Anna May Wong, who is a well-known actress!

"How much is the orange juice?" Anna May Wong asks.

"We are raising money for the children refugees in China. The opera tickets and flags are $1 each. Would you like to buy some?" I ask. Ruby just sits there, stunned.

Anna May Wong is impressed with our kind thoughts. She reaches for her Mandarin purse and flips open her wallet. She pulls out her checkbook and writes her donation to the United China Relief campaign.

"How many would you like?" I ask.

"Just one ticket and a flag, please."

After Anna May Wong leaves, Ruby and I look at the check with astonishment. It's for $300!

色鮮やかなムーン・フェスティバルに、ますます人が集まってきます。しばらくするとオレンジ・ジュースのスタンドは、のどが乾いた人の長い列ができました。そこへ見覚えのある顔が加わりました。ルビーと私はその顔を見ているうちハッとしました。それは、アナ・メイ・ウォングという有名な女優さんだったのです！

「オレンジ・ジュースはおいくら？」アナ・メイ・ウォングがたずねます。

「私達は中国の戦争被害者のために募金活動をしています。歌劇の切符とアメリカの国旗、それぞれ一ドルですが、いくつかお求め下さいませんか?」私が応対しました。ルビーはびっくりしたまま座り込んで声も出ません。

アナ・メイ・ウォングは私たちの思いやりある行為に感心したのでしょう。マンダリン製のバックに手を伸ばすとお財布を取り出し、小切手帳を開くと「総合中国救済募金へ寄付」と書き込んだのです。

「おいくつ差し上げましょうか?」と私がたずねると、

「切符一枚と旗を一つ下さい」という返事です。

アナ・メイ・ウォングが立ち去ってから、小切手を見た私とルビーは飛び上がるほどびっくりしました。なんと三百ドルという大金が書き込まれていたからです。

CHINESE DINNERS
FLAGS ORANGE JUICE
$1
OPERA TICKETS
OPERA TICKETS $1
UNITED CHINA RELIEF CAMPAIGN
Anna May Wong 1942
Pay to the order of China Relief $300 00/100
Three hundred dollars and 00/100
Anna May Wong

August 7, 1942

Dear Yayeko,

Today in China City we celebrated the Moon Festival and raised funds for the United China Relief campaign. I think about refugees in war-torn countries. I think about you being trapped in that camp, too. I was the top seller of the fundraising drive. My prizes are a $100 Chinese banquet gift certificate and a Chinese silk jacket. I'm saving the gift certificate for you as food and clothing have become scarce these days. I miss you a lot. I hope the war will end soon. And I hope you will come home next Chinese New Year wearing your new Chinese silk jacket. Don't stop writing.

Love,

Mei Ling Lee
Los Angeles China City, California

１９４２年８月７日

親愛 なるヤエコちゃんへ

きょう、チャイナ・シティではムーン・フェステバルをお祝いし、私 たちは総合 中国 救済 運動 のために募金をしました。私 は戦争による難民 のことをよく思い浮かべます。募金コンテストの最高額 を集めたのは私 でした。一等賞 は百 ドルの中華 レストラン 招待 券 と、中国 製 の絹 のジャケットです。この頃 は、食 料 も衣料 も減ってきたようなので、この招 待 券 はヤエコちゃんのために取っておきます。あなたがいなくてさびしくてなりません。戦争 が早く終わることを願うばかりです。ヤエコちゃんが 来年 の、チャイニーズ・ニューイヤーまでに帰宅して賞 品 の絹 の中国 製 ジャケット を着てくれたらどんなに素晴らしいでしょうか。欠かさずにお手紙下 さいね。

愛をこめて

メイリン・リー

チャイナ・シティ・ロサンゼルス、カリフォルニア 州

12-year-old Mei Ling Lee
(today known as Marian Leng) in China City.
チャイナ・シティのメイリン・リー、
十二 歳 当時。（現 在のマリアン・レング）

*Photo courtesy of University of Southern California.,
on behalf of the USC Special Collections.*

CHINESE NEW YEAR

1945

Author's Note

China City

In 1933, Old Chinatown was destroyed to make way for what was going to be Union Station, a major railroad terminal in downtown Los Angeles. Unfortunately, thousands of Chinese American residents were forced to relocate to crowded enclaves near the City Market on 9th and San Pedro Streets. The Chinese community and developers discussed many proposals and plans for a new Chinatown. Eventually, two separate settlements, new Chinatown and China City, were built in 1938.

China City was located adjacent to El Pueblo de Los Angeles, an area bounded by Spring Street on the west, Main Street on the east, Macy Street on the south and Ord Street on the north. China City was created primarily for tourism and was built with the support of Christine Sterling, a promoter of Olvera Street, and Harry Chandler, the publisher of *The Los Angeles Times*. Tourists could explore the "romance of the exotic Orient" by taking rickshaw rides for 25 cents and enjoy the traditional Chinese theater performed in English. China City depicted a mysterious Chinese village with curio shops, herb stores, temples and shrines, lotus pools, pagodas and popular restaurants. Displaced residents of the demolished Old Chinatown operated many businesses in China City.

The China City gateway on Ord Street with Union Station in background.
Photo courtesy of Harry Quillen Collection.

The China City gateway on North Main Street in 1938.
Photo courtesy of the SECURITY PACIFIC COLLECTION/ Los Angeles Public Library.

China City was also called Chinese Movie Land, with marketplace, rickshaws and replicas of life in China for the burgeoning Hollywood movie industry. Based on Pearl Buck's novel in 1940, the House of Wang set for the film *The Good Earth* was in China City. It was one of the first American movies that made any attempt to portray China and its people with sympathy. Chinese American workers in China City were called upon to act in many Hollywood motion pictures. Tom Gubbins was one of the Hollywood casting agents based in China City recruiting Chinese talent. Mei Ling Lee, Doris Chan, Frances Chan, Richard Sung Lee and Johnny Yee in this story had played various roles in many Hollywood films in the 1940s. Johnny Yee, who had several jobs in China City, thought it was funny that he had to learn Pidgin English in order to sound like he was Chinese. He, of course, was an all-American boy, although Chinese American. Anna May Wong was the first Chinese American actress to succeed in Hollywood, starring in many silent films in the 1920s and 1930s.

During the 1940s, China City was successful, with many thousands of visitors every year. It attracted a great deal of the city's attention. However, it was destroyed by a disastrous fire in 1949, and China City was never rebuilt. Today, a distinctive "Shanghai Street" neon sign on Ord Street is one of the few reminders of a once remarkable place. Although China City is demolished, its historic presence is fondly remembered by many Los Angeles elders.

Manzanar War Relocation Center

Japan attacked Pearl Harbor in Hawaii on December 7, 1941. Two months after this devastating event, President Franklin Roosevelt signed Executive Order 9066, which authorized the mass removal and incarceration of people of Japanese ancestry in the U.S., this due to so called "military necessity." Japanese Americans were believed to be potential spies for the Japanese government, and thought to pose a threat to national security. Without any proof of wrongdoing, close to 120,000 Japanese Americans were interned. About two-thirds of them were American citizens by birth. Manzanar, in the Owens Valley of California, was the first of ten War Relocation Centers across the U.S. during World War II. It had a population of approximately 11,000.

In 1983, the Commission on Wartime Relocation and Internment of Civilians, a congressional commission, finally declared that the internment was unjustified. The decision to incarcerate Japanese Americans was based on "race prejudice, war hysteria, and a failure of political leadership."

Today, Manzanar is designated a National Historic Site, and is visited by tens of thousands of people every year. The Manzanar legacy and the Japanese Americans who fought injustice to secure their constitutional rights should stand as a lesson to America to preserve human and civil rights of every person.

The real Yayeko Akiyama was actualy 15 years old when her family was uprooted and sent to the Poston War Relocation Center in 1942. Yayeko wrote many letters to her best friend Mei Ling Lee to recount her internment experience. However, Mei Ling did not receive any word from Yayeko after the war ended in 1945. Mei Ling, also known as Marian Leng today, is now in her eighties and hopes to see Yayeko again one day.

Entrance to the Manzanar War Relocation Center with the gatehouse in the background.
Photo courtesy of the Library of Congress, Ansel Adams, photographer, LC-DIG-ppprs-00226 DLC.

United China Relief

The Sino-Japanese War broke out in July 1937 in China. Japan launched a full-scale invasion of China, killing hundreds of thousands of Chinese civilians and soldiers. The war cut off Chinese Americans from their relatives in China. Horrifying reports of Japanese military atrocities in places like Nanking, the former capital city of China, galvanized Chinese American communities in the United States. To aid the suffering of war victims in China, United China Relief (UCR) held fundraising campaigns across the U.S. by organizing moon festivals, bazaars, fashion shows, and Chinese theatrical productions during World War II. The UCR fund was used to purchase food, medical and surgical supplies. By the end of World War II, the Chinese homeland was turned into a graveyard for an estimated 35 million innocents. The ethnic Chinese community in the U.S. raised a total of about $25 million for the war relief effort in China.

Lion dance at the Moon Festival to benefit the United China Relief.

Photo courtesy of the SECURITY PACIFIC COLLECTION/
Los Angeles Public Library

作者の覚え書き

チャイナ・シティ

　１９３３年、ロサンゼルスのダウンタウンで主要な鉄道ターミナルとなるユニオン駅の建設のため、旧チャイナ・タウンは取り壊されました。数多くの中国系アメリカ人は、不運なことに半ば強制的に九番街とサンペドロ通りにある市営マーケット近くの、すでに密集していた飛び地へと移動させられたのでした。中国系の地域団体と開発業者は、新しいチャイナ・タウンの建設プランを出し合い協議を重ねました。その結果、１９３８年に造成された新チャイナ・タウンと、チャイナ・シティに分かれて定着するようになったのです。

　チャイナ・シティは西側にスプリング街、東側にメイン街、南側はメイシー街、北側はオード街に囲まれエル・プエブロ・デ・ロサンゼルス地区に隣接していました。チャイナ・シティが建設された主な理由は観光目的で、オリベラ街のプロモーター、クリスティン・スティアリング、ロサンゼルス・タイムスの発行人、ハリー・チャンドラーが援助して完成しました。観光客は"東洋の異国情緒"を味わおうと２５セントの運賃を払って人力車に乗ったり、英語で演じられる中国の伝統的な演劇を探訪しに出かけたのです。チャイナ・シティは骨董品店、薬草店、お寺や神殿、蓮の池、仏塔、そして人気のあるレストランなどでミステリアスな中国の村落を演出しました。つぶされた旧チャイナ・タウンから追い出された住民の多くは、チャイナ・シティで商売をするようになります。

ユニオン駅を背景にしたオード通りのチャイナ・シティ入り口。

Photo courtesy of Harry Quillen Collectio.

１９３８年、北メイン通りのチャイナ・シティ入り口。
Photo courtesy of the SECURITY PACIFIC COLLECTION/
Los Angeles Public Library.

チャイナ・シティは発展するハリウッドの映画産業のために、商店街や人力車など中国の生活環境を真似て作られたため、チャイニーズ・ムービーランドとも呼ばれました。１９４０年のパール・バックの小説をもとに作られた映画「グッド・アース（大地）」のワング家のセットはチャイナ・シティの中にあります。この映画は中国とその国民を描写する上で、初めて心を通わせて作られたアメリカ製映画のひとつと言えます。チャイナ・シティで働く中国系アメリカ人は、ハリウッドの映画の多くに助演するよう求められました。トム・ガビンスはチャイナ・シティで中国人のタレントを斡旋する、ハリウッドの配役代理人の一人でした。メイリン・リー、ドリス・チャン、フランシス・チャン、リチャード・サング・リー、そしてジョニー・イーなどは、チャイナ・シティでのいくつかの撮影にかかわっています。本国の中国人であるかのごとく、なまりのある英語を話すよう訓練されたとは愉快な話です。彼らは中国系アメリカ人とはいえ、純粋なアメリカっ子です。アナ・メイ・ウォングは１９２０年から１９３０年代、多くの無声映画に出演し、ハリウッドで成功した最初の中国系アメリカ人の女優でした。

１９４０年代、チャイナ・シティは毎年、観光客で大いに賑わいました。町の魅力がものをいったのですが、残念ながら１９４９年の火災で見る影もなく壊滅してしまい、ついに再興されることはありませんでした。今日では、オード街で目を引く"上海ストリート"のネオンサインが、かってのはなやかだった頃を偲ぶ名残りのひとつとなっています。チャイナ・シティは跡形も無くなったとは言え、ロサンゼルスの年配の多くの人に歴史的な思い出として深い印象が残されているのです。

マンザナー戦時収容所

１９４１年１２月７日、日本軍はハワイのパール·ハーバーを攻撃しました。この衝撃的な事件の二ヶ月後、フランクリン·ルーズベルト大統領は大統領命令９０６６号を発令、アメリカに住む日本人の血を引くすべての人を"軍事的必要性"の理由で、強制的に立ち退かせ収監するよう命じました。日系アメリカ人は、日本政府のスパイになる可能性があると言われ、国家の安全をおびやかすと信じられたのです。犯罪となる何の証拠もないまま、約十二万人の日系人が抑留されました。全員のおよそ三分の二はアメリカ生まれの市民でした。カリフォルニア州 オーウェンズ·バレーのマンザナーは、第二次世界大戦でアメリカ全土に設けられた十の戦時収容所の最初の施設です。ここの収容人口は約一万一千人でした。

１９８３年、国会の委託を受けた「市民の戦時立ち退きと収監」に関する調査委員会は、ついに"強制収容は不正当であった"と公表します。日系アメリカ人を収監した主な理由は「人種差別」、「戦争によるヒステリー」、そして「政治的指導力の欠如」に起因すると結論しました。

今日では、マンザナーは国の史跡として指定され、毎年多くの人が訪れています。マンザナーの遺産と、憲法上の人間の権利を守るために不平等と戦った日系アメリカ人のことは、アメリカが人間の基本的権利を誰にでも保障する上で、教訓となるに違いありません。

実際では、アキヤマ·ヤエコさんは十五歳の時、１９４２年に家族とともにポストン戦時収容所に送られました。ヤエコさんは親友のメイリン·リーさんに、彼女の収容所生活について詳しく、たびたび手紙を書き送りました。しかし、１９４５年に終戦となったあと、メイリンさんへの音信は途絶えてしまいました。今日では、マリアン·レングさんとして知られるメイリンさんは、八十歳を越えておられますが、いつかヤエコさんと再会したいと願っています。

出入りの検問所が見えるマンザナー
戦時収容所への入り口
Photo courtesy of the Library of Congress,
Ansel Adams, photographer, LC-DIG-ppprs-00226 DLC.

総合中国救済運動

日中戦争は、1937年に中国で勃発しました。日本は中国へ大軍を派兵し、多くの市民や軍人を殺しました。戦争により中国系アメリカ人と、中国の家族は交流を絶たれてしまいます。中国の旧首都である南京における日本軍の非道な殺略のニュースなどは、アメリカに住む中国系アメリカ人にひどいショックを与えました。中国の戦災で苦しむ人々を救おうと、総合中国救済運動（UCR）は、第二次世界大戦中、アメリカ全土で中秋節、バザー、ファッション・ショー、そして劇の上演などを組織して、募金キャンペーンを行いました。この救済運動で得られた募金は、食料、医料品、そして外科手術用品などに使用されました。第二次世界大戦が終わる頃には、中国全土で推計三千五百万人の無垢の民が亡くなり、お墓だらけになったとされます。アメリカの中国系民族が、中国の戦争被災者の救済のために集めた募金総額は二千五百万ドルにのぼったと言われています。

総合中国救援活動で活躍した
ムーン・フェステバルのライオン・ダンス。

Photo courtesy of the SECURITY PACIFIC COLLECTION/
Los Angeles Public Library.

The east gateway of China City on Main and
Macy Streets, surrounded by a "Great Wall."

"グレイト・ウォール"に囲まれたメイン通りと
メイシー通りのチャイナ・シティ東側入り口。

Photo courtesy of Harry Quillen Collection.

Rickshaw driver Sinclair with Frances Chan in front of
Chung Dat Loo restaurant in China City.

チャイナ・シティの「チャング・ダット・ルー」中華レストラン前で、
人力車の車夫、シンクレアーとフランシス・チャン。

*Photo courtesy of University of Southern California.,
on behalf of the USC Special Collections.*

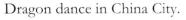

Dragon dance in China City.

チャイナ・シティのドラゴン・ダンス。

*Photo courtesy of "Seaver Center for Western History Research,
Los Angeles County Museum of Natural History.*

The Court of Four Seasons in China City with Golden Phoenix Restaurant and China City Gift Shop in the background.

「ゴールデン・フィニックス」と「チャイナ・シティ・ギフト・ショップ」が
背後に見えるチャイナ・シティのフォーシーズンズ広場。

*Photo courtesy of University of Southern California.,
on behalf of the USC Special Collections.*

Exterior view of the Chung Dat Loo restaurant owned
by Mei Ling Lee's parents in China City, 1940s.

１９４０年代、メイリン・リーの両親が経営した
「チャング・ダット・ルー」レストランの外観。

*Photo courtesy of the SECURITY PACIFIC COLLECTION/
Los Angeles Public Library.*

Gilbert and Donald Siu work as extras in the motion picture *The Good Earth*, based on Pearl Buck's novel, in 1940.

１９４０年、パール・バックの小説を元にした映画「グッド・アース（大地）」に脇役　として出演したギルバートとドナルド・シウ。

Photo courtesy of SHADES OF L.A. ARCHIVES/ Los Angeles Public Library.

Anna May Wong was the first Chinese American actress to succeed in Hollywood, starring in many silent films in the 1920s and 1930s.

アナ・メイ・ウォングは１９２０年から１９３０年代、多くの無声映画に出演し、ハリウッドで成功した最初の中国系アメリカ人の女優でした。

Photo courtesy of Johnny Yee Collection.

Tom Gubbins, a Hollywood casting agent, recruits Chinese extras to act as Japanese soldiers during World War II. Luke Chan was one of hundreds of Chinese American actors in 1942.

トム・ガビンスはハリウッドの配役代理業を営んだ。第二次世界大戦の際、中国人の俳優が日本人を代わりに演じた。１９４２年、ルーク・チャンは数多くいた中国系アメリカ人の俳優の一人。

Photo courtesy of Johnny Yee Collection.

Pearl Jean Wong enjoys a rickshaw ride
for 25 cents in China City.

チャイナ・シティの二十五(にじゅうご)セントが運賃(うんちん)の
人力車(じんりきしゃ)を楽(たの)しむパール・ジーン・ウォング。

Photo courtesy of University of Southern California.,
on behalf of the USC Special Collections.

The House of Wang set from the film *The Good Earth*
with actor John Wesley Luck in China City.

映画(えいが)「グッド・アース(大地)」に使用(しよう)された「ワングさんの家(いえ)」
のセットと俳優(はいゆう)ジョン・ウエスリー・ラック。

Photo courtesy of the SECURITY PACIFIC COLLECTION/
Los Angeles Public Library.

Pearl Jean Wong at the Kuan Yin
Temple in China City.

チャイナ・シティのクワン・イン
寺院でのパール・ジーン・ワング。

*Photo courtesy of University of Southern California., on behalf of the
USC Special Collections.*

Kuan Yin Temple in China City.

チャイナ・シティのクワン・イン寺院。

Photo courtesy of Harry Quillen Collection.

16-year-old Johnny Yee at the Kuan Yin
Temple in China City, 1941.

1941年、チャイナ・シティのクワン・イン
寺院でのジョニー・イー、十六歳。

Photo courtesy of Johnny Yee Collection.

Wong A. Loy and "Peanut Man" demonstrate
martial arts in China City.

ウォング・A・ロイと "ピーナッツマン"
によるチャイナ・シティでの武道演技。
ぶどうえんぎ

*Photo courtesy of University of Southern California.,
on behalf of the USC Special Collections.*

The Court of Lotus Pools in China City. From left to right,
holding umbrellas: Dorothy Lam, Doris Chan and Ethel Wong.

チャイナ・シティの蓮池広場で、左から傘をさしている
はすいけひろば　ひだり　かさ
ドロシー・ラム、ドリス・チャンとエシール・ウォング。

*Photo courtesy of University of Southern California., on behalf of the
USC Special Collections.*

Members of a Chinese band perform in China City.
From left to right: "Peanut Man," Paul Fung, Mr. Tsin
Nam Ling, Victor Wong, Wong Loy, and Ruby Ling.

チャイナ・シティで演奏する中国音楽隊の人たち。
左から右へ、"ピーナッツマン"のポール・ファング、
ツイン・ナム・リングし、ビクター・ウォング、ウォング・
ロイ、そしてルビー・リング。

*Photo courtesy of the SECURITY PACIFIC COLLECTION/
Los Angeles Public Library.*

Doris and Frances Chan play the butterfly harp at the
Moon Festival in China City, circa 1940.

１９４０年頃、チャイナ・シティのムーン・フェステバルで
「バタフライ・ハープ」を演じたドリスとフランシス・チャン。

*Photo courtesy of the SECURITY PACIFIC COLLECTION/
Los Angeles Public Library.*

Chinese women's band in China City. From left to right:
Dorothy Sue, Pearl Jean Wong, unknown, Lillian Luck.

チャイナ・シティの中国女性音楽隊。左から右へ、
ドロシー・スー、パール・ジーン・ウォング、氏名不詳、
リリアン・ラック。

*Photo courtesy of "Seaver Center for Western History Research,
Los Angeles County Museum of Natural History.*

China City was destroyed by fire in early 1939. Some of the businesses
had to relocate to New Chinatown. However, China City was soon rebuilt.

ねんしょとう　　　　　　　　かさい　かいめつ　　　　　　　　　　　しん
1939 年 初頭 、チャイナ・シティは火災で壊 滅 。いくつかのビジネスは新 チャイナ・
　　　いてん　よぎ　　　　　　　　　　　　　　　　　　　　　　さいけん
タウンに移転を余儀なくされる。しかし、チャイナ・シティはすぐ再 建 された。

Photo courtesy of the SECURITY PACIFIC COLLECTION/
Los Angeles Public Library.

Theatrical actors wearing traditional
opera costumes on stage in China City.

でんとうてきかげき
チャイナ・シティで伝 統 的 歌劇の
いしょう　ぶたい　た　はいゆう
衣 装 で舞台に立つ俳 優 たち。

Photo courtesy of the SECURITY PACIFIC COLLECTION/
Los Angeles Public Library.

To the victims of wars past and present. And to my husband Michael
and daughters Crystal and Celena for their endless support.
- I.S.

To Jake Lee, my first watercolor instructor, and my five grandchildren— Bryce, Austin, Grant, Ashley and Q.
I hope they grow up to appreciate all cultures as much as I do.
- G.G.R.

Text copyright © 2008 by Icy Smith
Illustrations copyright © 2008 by Gayle Garner Roski
Japanese translation copyright © 2008 by East West Discovery Press

Published by:
East West Discovery Press
P.O. Box 3585, Manhattan Beach, CA 90266
Phone: 310-545-3730, Fax: 310-545-3731
Website: www.eastwestdiscovery.com

Written by Icy Smith
Illustrated by Gayle Garner Roski
Japanese translation by Sunny Seki
Japanese proofreading by Hazuki Kataoka and Haruko Sakakibara
Edited by Marcie Rouman
Design and production by Luzelena Rodriguez and Icy Smith

Author's Acknowledgement:
Special thanks to Marian Leng, who shared her personal story with me for the basis of this book, and to Celena Smith, Yee Lew and Justin A. for their
assistance on creating the illustrated characters. Special thanks also to Carolyn Cole of the Los Angeles Public Library, Photography Collection; Carol Duan
of the Chinatown Public Library; Dace Taube of the University of Southern California, Special Collections; and Betty Uyeda of the Seaver Center for
Western History Research, Los Angeles County Museum of Natural History for their assistance on my photography research. Last but not least, I gratefully
acknowledge Gayle Garner Roski for her awesome watercolor paintings.

All rights reserved. No part of this book may be reproduced, translated, or transmitted in any form or by any means, graphic, electronic, or mechanical,
including photocopying, recording, taping, or by any information storage or retrieval systems, without the permission in writing from the publisher. Requests
for permission or further information should be addressed to:
East West Discovery Press, P.O. Box 3585, Manhattan Beach, CA 90266.

ISBN-13: 978-0-9799339-6-7 Hardcover
Library of Congress Control Number: 2007937883
First Bilingual English and Japanese Edition 2008
Printed in China
Published in the United States of America

Mei Ling in China City is also available in English only and four bilingual editions including
English with Chinese, Japanese, Spanish and Vietnamese.